A DAY WELL SPENT

Robert O. Martichenko

Illustrations by Blueberry Illustrations

A Day Well Spent
By Robert O. Martichenko

ISBN: 978-0-9970308-5-3

Blueberry Illustrations is a world class illustrations and self publishing company for children's books and other books. The illustrators of Blueberry Illustrations are recipients of various awards and nominations. More than 350 books have been illustrated and published by the company and many more are in the process.
www.blueberryillustrations.com

DEDICATION

To Emilee and Abigail,
May we take many walks together
and enjoy *A Day Well Spent*.

One Thing
*There's only one thing
I need in this world.
It's the love I receive
From my two little girls.*

I'd really like
To take a hike,
Around a lake I've never seen.

One without
A person about,
So I could wander while I dream.

Then in time
Perhaps I'd find
Some friends for company.

We would talk
And go for walks.
Many different lives we'd see.

I can imagine
Meeting a badger.
We'd burrow through her home.

To hear the sound
Of life underground,
To feel happiness that she's known.

A little warm den
The family defends
Against any unfriendly passerby.

Buried in winter
By branches that splinter,
In spring, her young open their eyes.

Then I'd stop
And sit on a rock
To grab a little snack.

Out of the woods
Would come the masked hoods,
Raccoons on their gentle attack.

Sharing my lunch
To learn a bunch
About a bandit's unlawful ways.

They'd want me to hang
With the roving gang,
An outlaw the rest of my days.

That afternoon
I'd swim with a loon.
She'd introduce me to her mate.

Surrounding the eggs
She'd secretly laid,
We'd worry about their fate.

With no problem at all
I'd master the call,
To sing thru the day's last light.

Nature would listen
As soft ripples glistened
Across the lake as the two took flight.

As the sun went down
I'd look around
For a soft place to spend the night.

The dusk would smile
With the music of the wild,
Entire worlds just beyond my sight.

Sitting by the fire
Enjoying feeling tired,
The crackling at my feet.

To think again
I could meet new friends
And offer them a seat.

In from the dark,
With a high-pitched hark,
Would be the oldest, wisest owl.

We'd talk of the world,
The problems incurred,
Offer solutions with a quiet growl.

I'd feel like a fool
And ask where she schooled,
A question she'd have to ponder.

And the moment she'd leave
It would be easy to see
The many things left to wonder.

After saying goodbye
To the stars in the sky,
I'd fall into a well-needed sleep.

Dreaming of places
With rosy glowing faces
Around me, busy little beavers would eat.

The moon sending its glare
Within the fresh air,
My skin soaking it in for hours.

The forest internal
To life that's nocturnal,
Breezes showing off their powers.

Just before dawn
I'd awake to a fawn,
Her mother, and dad, the buck.

In search of fresh leaves
We'd skip through the trees,
Ever grateful for our luck.

Then in the sky
Majestically flying by,
An optimistic and peaceful bird.

My heart would feel love
With the sight of the dove
And the message heard in its word.

Yes, I think I'd like
To take a hike,
Around a lake I've never seen.

One without
A person about,
So I could wander while I dream.

Maybe then
After meeting new friends,
I would start to understand.

The world belongs
To everyone,
And no one owns the land.

Robert O. Martichenko is a Canadian-American entrepreneur, writer, poet, public speaker, and podcaster. On a perfect day, Robert can be found hiking in the mountains with his family, friends, and faithful yellow Labrador Retrievers. Robert is interested in making the world a better place by focusing on stories that promote kindness, respect, and empathy.

Robert is also an award-winning novelist.

A Day Well Spent is a poem written by Robert O. Martichenko originally published in his novel **Drift and Hum**.

Drift and Hum is a captivating novel about the kite ride of life and dealing with obstacles along the way. The story is told through the eyes of Sam, a 50-year-old South Carolina man who reflects from the present day back to his Canadian childhood to make sense of all the challenges and universal entropy he has faced. His journey includes an extraordinary bond and friendship with three other boys as the four "Beaver Brothers" embark on adventure after adventure in their quest for peace of mind in the Canadian North and the American South.

Learn more at www.driftandhum.com